Kayak

by Jordan Hall

A SAMUEL FRENCH ACTING EDITION

SAMUEL FRENCH

FOUNDED 1830

NEW YORK HOLLYWOOD LONDON TORONTO

SAMUELFRENCH.COM

ISBN 978-0-573-69947-4   Printed in U.S.A.   #29897

MUSIC USE NOTE

Licensees are solely responsible for obtaining formal written permission from copyright owners to use copyrighted music in the performance of this play and are strongly cautioned to do so. If no such permission is obtained by the licensee, then the licensee must use only original music that the licensee owns and controls. Licensees are solely responsible and liable for all music clearances and shall indemnify the copyright owners of the play and their licensing agent, Samuel French, Inc., against any costs, expenses, losses and liabilities arising from the use of music by licensees.

IMPORTANT BILLING AND CREDIT
REQUIREMENTS

All producers of *KAYAK must* give credit to the Author of the Play in all programs distributed in connection with performances of the Play, and in all instances in which the title of the Play appears for the purposes of advertising, publicizing or otherwise exploiting the Play and/or a production. The name of the Author *must* appear on a separate line on which no other name appears, immediately following the title and *must* appear in size of type not less than fifty percent of the size of the title type.

KAYAK was initially developed as a monologue in a Playwrighting Masterclass at the Tarragon Theatre in December of 2008. Early drafts were presented in a reading at Women Playwrights International in Mumbai, India in November of 2009, and as part of Tableau d'Hôte Theatre's Series of New Canadian Works in Montreal in December of 2009.

KAYAK was first performed in The Theatre Passe Muraille Backspace on August 6th, 2010 as an official selection of the 2010 Summerworks Festival in Toronto, Ontario. The director was Tommy Taylor; the producers were Julian DeZotti and Tara Yelland; Gin Shulist stage-managed. The cast was as follows:

ANNIE . . . . Rosemary Dunsmore

PETER . . . . Daniel Briere

JULIE . . . . Dienye Waboso

KAYAK was the winner of the 2010 Samuel French Canadian Playwrights Competition and the The PGC's Post-Secondary Playwrighting Contest.

CHARACTERS

ANNIE IVERSEN – a suburban housewife. Various ages, mostly fifty-six.

PETER IVERSEN – a recent university graduate. Various ages, mostly twenty-four

JULIE DANIELS – a Greenpeace activist. Various ages, mostly twenty-three.

AUTHOR'S NOTES

(Dear Reader: If you can bring yourself to wait, I would prefer you read these notes after the play. Because, when you get down to it, the play is what I meant to say, and how I meant to say it.)

Kayak began as a simple writing exercise. Late in 2008 – an unseasonably wet and cold year in Toronto – I was infuriated by conversations I'd have with Climate Change deniers. The sort of people who, despite irrefutable scientific evidence, pretend we aren't having an effect on the planet. I decided to conjure one up and make her explain herself: and there was Annie Iversen.

The kayak came later. As Annie explained why she'd refused to see it coming, and her frustrations coalesced around her son's girlfriend Julie and Julie's overtly left-wing politics, a few more of my infuriations wound their way into Annie's life:

First, there was Rachel Corrie, upon whom Julie's character had been modeled, and the furor that surrounded her death. It seemed to me, as people labeled her misguided or naïve, or segued into the Israeli/ Palestinian debate, that they were either missing or deliberately avoiding the point: Here was a girl who had given up her safety and her comfort to help others. Who believed that it was "a good idea for us all to drop everything and devote our lives to making this [injustice] stop" (Corrie 49). Rachel is a reproach to those of us who just go on with our lives as though horrors are not happening in the world, and it seemed we would use any excuse we could find to avoid looking directly at that fact.

My second infuriation was the re-election of Stephen Harper in October of 2008. Despite Harper's disastrous fiscal showing and obvious contempt for social programs, the Canadian public didn't like Stephane Dion's image, and so they ignored an obviously superior political platform – or three. The idea that we had allowed how pleasant or comforting a person seemed to be affect our assessment of whether the things he was promoting were logical, beneficial or even ethical, terrified me.

These, strangely enough, led to the kayak. It was Julie's. Like Rachel, Julie is a figure of activism, feminism and ethical superiority. Julie, and by extension the kayak, is a reproach to Annie. She's uncompromising and she's right, but no one will listen to her because no one can stand her.

*(This, by the way, is the point where you should **really** stop reading, because I'm going to talk about the end of the play. At least you've been warned.)*

And so Annie came to be stranded alone on the water, finally able to recognize Julie because she was now literally in the same boat. But was she stalking Peter and Julie during a protest? Had a camping trip gone wrong? Something had happened to force Annie to see Julie. To recognize her as good. To recognize her as a daughter. And suddenly I was sure it had happened too late. The world had ended. A flood. And this is how I came to Noah, because poor Annie Iversen was alone in an Ark of One.

Invariably, after a reading of *Kayak*, someone will try to explain to me why they dislike the way Peter comes to love Julie because she's good, or because she's right. I've been told repeatedly that people don't fall in love with someone's ideals or morals. I cannot disagree more. I hope people leave this play with the thought that good – rigorous, deep good, the kind that isn't easy – isn't just something we should pay lip service to. It is exactly what we should love people for. Because if we cannot come to understand that, if we cannot do better than we have, then there's nothing left to do but wait for the flood.

(Thanks.)

Jordan Hall, February 2011.

Reference:
Corrie, Rachel. *My Name is Rachel Corrie.* Katharine Viner and Alan Rickman, ed. New York: TCG, 2005.

ACKNOWLEDGEMENTS

There are a great many people to thank for the two-year journey of writing this play. Thanks (in chronological order) belong to: Brian Quirt at the Tarragon; Rosemary Doyle & Carol MacLennan with The Alumnae Theatre's NPD; David Copelin; Bryan Wade and Martin Kinch at UBC; The International Playwrights of WPI Mumbai; Cassandra Rose & Tableau D'Hôte Theatre; Hope MacIntyre and Sarasvati Transformative; Dave Deveau, Cameron D. Mackenzie and Heidi Taylor at the PTC; and most especially Julian Dezotti, Tara Yelland and Tommy Taylor with the Original Norwegian, for believing in the script long before it became the script.

A SPECIAL NOTE

For Environmental Groups considering staging amateur productions of *Kayak* as fundraisers: Please contact the playwright at www.jordanhall.ca, as she has made provisions for the donation of her portion of the play's royalties back to your organization, provided your group and the proposed production match certain criteria.

For Rachel Corrie, and every activist like her –
brave enough to change our world by saying:
"This comes first."

For David and Tommy and Julian and Cassandra –
and always, always, my mother.

(Darkness. The sound of water against a fiberglass hull. A woman's voice hums snatches of Who Built the Ark?[1] *The darkness becomes the blue light of early morning.)*

*(**ANNIE IVERSEN**, a tall woman with peroxide blonde hair, sits centre stage in a large kayak. She is slumped over, drifting in and out of sleep. The kayak should sit on a riser, or blocks, to keep **ANNIE** at waist height. During the course of the play, unless specifically noted, **ANNIE** does not leave the kayak.)*

*(The light grows. **ANNIE** wakes and scans her surroundings. Whatever she's looking for, she doesn't find it.)*

ANNIE. I don't like kayaks. They're unstable. One second you're sitting there, the next you're upside down and underwater.

(During the following speech she takes out a packet of chocolate, a bag of marshmallows, and a sleeve of graham crackers. She makes herself a S'more.)

This one was my son Peter's. Peter's not much of a kayaker either. Or – he wasn't. He took it up because of Julie. Julie had this tiny little kayak, barely longer than she was. She could roll that thing over as easily as you turn a steering wheel. So fast you'd wonder how she'd have time to get wet. Not that it would matter if Julie got wet, because Julie doesn't wear make-up or believe in hair products.

(It's the last marshmallow. This hits her. She crumples up the empty marshmallow bag to stow it, pauses, then tosses it into the water.)

Or littering. *(She has a little chuckle about that.)* In case you're wondering, I don't really like Julie much, either.

*(**ANNIE** eats the S'more as she keeps speaking.)*

9

ANNIE. *(cont.)* I thought she was a phase Pete was going through. He'd had Susan (his goth phase), and Terri (his actress phase) – Julie was just his politically correct phase. She was the sort of girl who floated around the world spraying Japanese whaling boats with firehoses, planting trees, and making perfectly nice people uncomfortable at parties.

*(**ANNIE** considers the chocolate and graham crackers. She'd like to eat more, but she puts them away.)*

Once she stopped being new and exciting, Pete was supposed to move on to another phase. Possibly some kind of marry-a-nice-girl-with-hobbies-that-didn't-involve-the-Japanese-government-pressing-charges phase. And that would have been that.

*(**ANNIE** pulls out a half-full Evian bottle, takes a short swallow, and carefully stows it again. This done, she unsnaps a GPS beacon from against the side of the kayak. She taps at it, shakes it.)*

GPS my ass. It would take a miracle to find anything with one of these goddamn things. The one in the BMW tells you which way to turn and how far to drive, which becomes more important than you'd think as you get older. Julie'd probably think this is hilarious. Stupid old Mrs. Iversen lost on the Credit River like Noah in the Ark.

*(**ANNIE** reattaches the GPS beacon. During the following she takes out a traveller's toothbrush and brushes her teeth with water at the side of the kayak.)*

At least *he* had company. *(beat)* You know you're in a mess when biblical disaster starts sounding preferable. And Noah never had to deal with a post-third wave eco-feminist. Lucky bastard. *(She puts away the toothbrush.)* From the first mention of "Global Citzenship," you just knew she was going to be trouble.

*(**PETER IVERSEN**,[2] a tall boy of twenty, enters right with a cellphone to his ear. He paces upstage right, then downstage right.)*

PETER. Still no answer from campus tours. I can't believe this.

ANNIE. Well, if the staff can't even be bothered to show you around, maybe –

PETER. Mom. I'm twenty. I can't live at home forever.

ANNIE. I know, I know. I just don't want you in some awful little place, sweetheart. The stress could disrupt your studies.

PETER. It's a business degree. It's not rocket science. *(under his breath:)* Or any science, really.

ANNIE. Peter.

PETER. What?

ANNIE. Don't be down on yourself. You've worked for this. Your father and I are proud of you.

PETER. Yeah. No. I know how much this means to you guys. *(He kisses her on the cheek.)* Look, would you mind waiting a sec in case someone actually shows? I'm gonna take one last shot at finding a hall rep.

(He exits up right.)

*(**ANNIE** gives the dormitory surroundings a good once-over. She isn't pleased with what she sees.)*

*(From offstage comes a peal of laughter. **JULIE DANIELS**, nineteen, a tiny girl in pigtails and cargo pants, emerges upstage left. She's damp. She walks backwards, calling out to someone offstage:)*

JULIE. No. Carruthers'll push the paper until we get back. So we'll go. We'll go and IWL can choke on us. I'll catch you tonight –

*(She's backed right into **ANNIE**.)*

JULIE. Oh. Oh my gosh – Sorry. I didn't see you.

ANNIE. Of course not. *(She's got a damp spot where **JULIE** touched her.)* How did you get so – ?

JULIE. Wet? We do this thing at the harbour. Race kayaks. To raise awareness about runoff pollution. *(She gives a shake, accidentally spraying **ANNIE** with more water.)*

ANNIE. Runoff pollution. Lovely.

JULIE. Are you touring with someone, Ms. – ?

ANNIE. *Mrs.* Iversen.

JULIE. Mrs. Iversen. Because this isn't a frosh floor.

ANNIE. A what?

JULIE. A freshman floor. If you're checking out rooms for your kid, they're down on one and two. The whole "Finally free from Mom and Dad; Sex, drugs and rock and roll" thing works better on all sides if it's far away from the seniors.

ANNIE. Oh. Oh no. My son *isn't* – and he won't be staying –

(**PETER** *returns.*)

PETER. No joy, Mom. I can't find – *(He takes in* **JULIE.** *They're on opposite sides of the kayak.)* – anybody. Uh – Hi.

JULIE. Hi. A little old for frosh, aren't you?

PETER. Third year. Actually.

JULIE. And you brought your mom with you?

PETER. Oh dear god, you've met.

ANNIE. Peter. Don't be a smart-aleck. This young woman –

JULIE. Julie.

ANNIE. Julie and I were talking about her charitable works. She kayaks for water pollution. Against water pollution.

PETER. Cool. Closest I've ever been to protesting was second grade. I refused to get off my skateboard when recess ended.

JULIE. A born rebel, huh?

PETER. Detention for the rest of the week, but they couldn't break me.

ANNIE. Stop that. He's modest, but he's starting his third year at the Rotman business school.

(*beat*)

JULIE. Rotman? Wow. And you look like such a nice boy.

PETER. Hey. I have facets. I'm not *just* a soulless capital-ist. I'll have you know I've been considering doing a minor in bio – / maybe ecology –

ANNIE. A minor in – ? Peter you haven't /said –

PETER. It's just something I was thinking about, Mom. I'm not switching programs.

JULIE. Too bad. I think a degree in ecology is damn sexy in a man. *(They laugh.* **ANNIE** *doesn't.)* The faculty at Rotman think that environmental action means selling organic juice to yuppies.

ANNIE. That hardly seems fair. Of course they have a busi-ness perspective.

JULIE. Uh – Yeah.

PETER. Are you in Ecology? Or Poli-Sci or something?

JULIE. No. I just know some people. If you're interested there's a meeting tonight – IWL is diverting the Tuichi[3] river in Bolivia and we're part of the interna-tional campaign to stop them.

PETER. Oh. Yeah –

JULIE. Some of us are gonna be part of a Greenpeace dem-onstration – we'll shoot the rapids. Try to get some media attention. If they do divert it, we'll be the last people to ever run the river.

PETER. That's amazing.

ANNIE. And this sort of thing doesn't interfere with school?

JULIE. Well, yeah. A little.

ANNIE. And the expense. And the *danger*.

JULIE. No one said doing the right thing was going to be painless, Mrs. Iversen.

*(***PETER*** absorbs that.)*

ANNIE. Well. Then. It's been a pleasure meeting you, Julie. But since there's no one here to take us on our tour, Peter and I/ had better –

JULIE. I could show him around. If you like? I'm the hall rep for this floor.

PETER. Must be fate. The girl I've been looking for all along.

(**JULIE** *smiles.*)

Y'know, Mom, you really don't have to stay here waiting for me. Why don't you take the car? I'll catch a bus back.

JULIE. Don't worry, Mrs. Iversen. I'll keep him safe and sound.

(**PETER** *and* **JULIE** *move upstage to the back wall. At the back of the stage, or in the wings post-its, markers, banner making supplies and a pair of stepladders are waiting.* **PETER** *and* **JULIE** *begin fixing banners and post-its to the back wall. They flirt silently as they work.*)

ANNIE. I definitely couldn't stand her.* Four years and she never stopped calling me *Mrs.* Iversen. The next time I saw Julie, she was on Peter's laptop. He was home for Christmas and he had video of the little nitwit kayaking down that river as part of her protest. She'd actually gone. There she was, paddling that tiny boat down rapids so big you'd have thought she was suicidal. And Peter had that gleam in his eye. The same one he had when he first saw the boys jumping off the ramps at the skateboard park, and you knew it was going to take twelve bloody noses and a broken wrist before he'd listen to you about what a bad idea this all was. Then he refused to eat the turkey because it wasn't certified cruelty-free, free-range and organic. Herb and I ate turkey sandwiches for two weeks to finish the leftovers.

(*Upstage,* **PETER** *and* **JULIE** *continue to silently add post-its and banners to the back wall when they are not active in* **ANNIE**'*s memory.*)

Now I recognize that what Julie was doing was – good. Or – right. I know about greenhouse gases. I recycle. I do everything I'm supposed to do. I even saw that movie with Al Gore and the big PowerPoint presentation.[4] I respected that she was trying to make the world a better place. But what I don't do is walk around as

---

* See Appendix A

though the place I grew up in is Sodom and Gomorrah, and I'm waiting for the flood that's going to cleanse the earth of scum.

(JULIE looks back over her shoulder.)

JULIE. You've got that confused, Mrs. Iversen.

ANNIE. You're going to correct me now too?

JULIE. Sodom and Gomorrah came after the flood.

ANNIE. Well, pardon me very much. If you're going to correct me you could at least have the decency to get me out of this mess.

(During the last, the morning light has been getting brighter. ANNIE squints into it. JULIE drifts downstage towards the kayak.)

JULIE. I'm more interested in keeping this little yarn honest.

(JULIE leans on the side of the kayak. It wobbles. ANNIE doesn't like that.)

ANNIE. Dying of exposure on some ridiculous parody of a camping trip isn't honest enough for you?

JULIE. Mmm. How long has it been now? A week?

ANNIE. Six days. This is the sixth day.

JULIE. Think someone'll find you before it hits forty? *(beat)* You want help, Mrs. Iversen? Sunstroke can cause hallucinations. You might wanna cover up.

(JULIE releases the kayak with a wobble and heads back upstage to PETER.)

ANNIE. I'm working on my tan.

(ANNIE waits until she's sure JULIE's gone, then pulls out a pair of sunglasses and a headscarf and puts them on. She looks around, decides on a direction, and starts paddling.)

(Behind ANNIE, the motion of her paddling sets JULIE and PETER in motion. As ANNIE speaks they move downstage, playing out a series of scenes from the past around ANNIE in the kayak:)

(**JULIE** *is distributing pamphlets.* **PETER** *sees* **JULIE**, *comes closer to talk. They chat, and* **JULIE** *makes a "Call Me" motion.* **PETER** *'s puzzled. He doesn't have her number.* **JULIE** *shakes her head and gives him a flyer.*)

ANNIE. *(cont.)* I did my best to like her. I honestly did. But sometimes she'd be over for dinner and it was all you could do not to slap her in the face.

(**ANNIE** *paddles harder. In the past,* **JULIE** *and* **PETER** *hoist placards for a protest.* **JULIE** *is very serious, but* **PETER** *only has eyes for* **JULIE**.)

And, yes, I'm sure the lamb was tortured and the emissions from transporting the fruit from Argentina were excessive and we were supporting Coke's abuse of child labour in third world countries by drinking soft drinks and the excess waste we were producing has doomed the world environment to a catastrophic meltdown.

(**ANNIE** *paddles as hard as she can. In the past,* **JULIE** *and* **PETER** *are both distributing flyers now. They see each other.* **PETER** *waves.* **JULIE** *waves. As a joke, they each give each other a flyer.* **JULIE** *gives* **PETER** *a peck on the cheek, laughs. Beat.* **PETER** *grabs* **JULIE** *and gives her a serious kiss. Flyers spill everywhere. They exit upstage right.*)

But people have lives and habits and comfort foods and places they need to go. And that doesn't change because you make them feel guilty and uncomfortable. You can't just force them. You can't just take away someone's son.

(**ANNIE** *'s exhausted. She stops to rest, mopping at her brow with her sleeves.*)

(**JULIE** *re-enters. Her hair is askew. She's wearing a camisole and carrying her shirt.*)

Julie?

(*Surprised,* **JULIE** *shrieks.* **ANNIE** *shrieks.* **PETER** *comes running out, without a shirt.*)

PETER. What the – *(sees his mother)* Oh god. *(He darts back into his room.)*

*(*JULIE *drops her face into her hands. Her shirt is still in them. She pulls it on.)*

ANNIE. Julie. What a surprise. That you're here. So early this morning.

JULIE. My thoughts exactly.

ANNIE. I thought you were off somewhere protesting the Olympics.

JULIE. Human rights violations in Tibet,[5] Mrs. Iversen. I had a few things to handle here on campus before – *(She realizes how that sounds.)* I mean – obviously not handling – I was dropping a few courses.

ANNIE. Oh. Something you didn't like this semester?

JULIE. All of it, actually.

ANNIE. All – ? You're leaving school?

*(*PETER *re-emerges, now with a shirt. He gives his mother a hug. Over* ANNIE*'s shoulder he mouths, "Sorry!" to* JULIE.*)*

PETER. Hi Mom. What are you doing here? At nine on a Saturday?

ANNIE. Some of your mail got delivered to the house. I thought you might need it.

*(*ANNIE *hands him a handful of envelopes.)*

PETER. Wow. Thanks. *(beat)* And you opened it for me too.

ANNIE. I thought I'd show your father your fall course schedule.

PETER. Oh.

ANNIE. Imagine our surprise.

PETER. I was going to tell you.

ANNIE. Organisms in their Environment? Conservation Biology?

PETER. It's just a few credits to make up a minor. I'll take a few courses in the summer and graduate in September.

ANNIE. It's an extra semester. We agreed that you wouldn't –

PETER. No, Mom. You agreed.

ANNIE. You certainly agreed to letting your father and I pay for all of this.

JULIE. It's just a few courses.

ANNIE. I'm sorry, Julie – but this is a family matter.

PETER. Mom, don't.

JULIE. Hey. I'm proud that Peter's taking an interest in his ethical existence.

(beat)

ANNIE. His ethical existence? The implication being that the path his father and I have laid out for him is *unethical*?

PETER. No. Mom. No one is saying that.

ANNIE. Don't think I don't know exactly why you're doing this, Peter. Your father and I aren't going to pay for you to flit around the world on an adventure tour disguised as social work. No offense meant, obviously.

JULIE. Oh. Obviously. You'd really do that, wouldn't you? Cut him off for wanting to be something other than a yuppie drone.

PETER. Jules. It's okay. I'll talk it out with them. Maybe it won't be a minor – maybe I'll just take Bio 150 as my last elective instead.

ANNIE. We just want to make sure you graduate on time.

JULIE. You're really going to let them run your life like this?

PETER. They're my parents –

JULIE. You hate your courses –

PETER. I can't pay for it without their help –

JULIE. And that's the deciding factor?

ANNIE. Oh for goodness sakes – of course it is. And it's a shame you don't have parents or someone with a lick of sense to stop you from dropping out and throwing your life away too!

(beat)

JULIE. Real nice. Good luck "talking it out" with her, Pete.

PETER. Jules!

(**JULIE** *exits upstage left.*)

She's taking a leave to spend six months with Greenpeace.

ANNIE. Oh. *(beat)* Oh dear. Well, I didn't mean that –

PETER. We can talk about this later, okay?

(**PETER** *runs after* **JULIE**.)

ANNIE. Not that she ever went back to school. First it was an extension of her "leave of absence." Then an "indefinite leave." She'd be here for a few months, then off on the next campaign. And never mind abandoning her education or wasting her life: It was a wonder she wasn't killed. That slip of a girl with her pretty face, standing there judging you like Solomon himself. That attitude in front of Indonesian riot police,[6] and crooked bureaucrats in the Philippines,[7] and U.S. army contractors in Okinawa[8] and their fingers must have been itching for the billy clubs.

(The day has become incredibly bright. **ANNIE** *takes off her headscarf and sunglasses and mops her brow.)*

(As **ANNIE** *keeps speaking,* **PETER** *and* **JULIE** *return to the back wall.* **JULIE** *keeps adding post-its, but* **PETER** *now wears a suit and carries a paper coffee cup. He faces front, working on the exchange floor. He waves at* **JULIE**. **JULIE** *joins him, takes away his coffee cup and replaces it with a reusable thermos.* **PETER** *smiles and loosens his tie. Together, they go back to work on the wall.)*

Not that I cared what sort of danger the pest flung herself into. But it was hard for Peter. Knowing that she might be in trouble, or hurt, and not being able to do anything about it. I waited for the stress and the distance to bring the whole silly thing to its natural conclusion, but every few months, there she was again. Dragging him off on camping trips or down to the harbour to splash around in sea kayaks, and always with new opinions about our "selfish" lives. No meat. No corn. Nothing from further than 100 miles away. Public transit. No new clothes. You had to agree, there was nothing to do but agree – but Dear God, it was just – exhausting. Peter was losing weight just trying to keep up with it all. He'd finished his degree – on schedule and with honours – and took a job as an assistant at his father's firm. I thought he might come home and commute with Herb, but instead he took an apartment in the city. Julie was there when she wasn't putting herself into life-threatening situations to protest palm kernel oil and the like. For awhile, she looked for a permanent placement with some local non-profit, but it never quite happened. Even the people who were supposed to agree with her couldn't stand her.

(**ANNIE** *takes out the half-full Evian bottle and looks at it, weighing whether or not to drink.*)

(**JULIE** *leaves the back wall and moves towards* **ANNIE** *in the kayak again.*)

JULIE. Don't hold back, now.

ANNIE. I'm sorry. Have I omitted some critical detail? Mixed a metaphor?

JULIE. Poor insufferable Julie, unreasonable Julie, fanatical Julie –

(**JULIE** *leans on the kayak beside* **ANNIE**. *The kayak wobbles.*)

ANNIE. Stop that. I'm in no rush for my first Eskimo roll.

JULIE. Julie, Julie, Julie. (**JULIE** *rocks the kayak in time with her speech.*) I'm hearing a lot about Julie. Not so much about Peter. Why do you think that is?

(**ANNIE** *bats her away from the side of the boat.*)

ANNIE. Oh for goodness sakes. Who knows? Maybe I'm dehydrated. (**ANNIE** *shakes the Evian bottle at* **JULIE**.) I'm sure you appreciate the karmic justice. (*She puts the water away without drinking.*)

JULIE. You really think I'm happy about that?

(**ANNIE** *turns to* **JULIE**. *Unnoticed, the headscarf and sunglasses slip off into the water.*)

ANNIE. I think that mercy wasn't your strong suit.

JULIE. Mercy only helps the guilty.

ANNIE. And you wonder why no one could stand to be in a room with you for more than ten minutes?

JULIE. You're the one who keeps conjuring me up. Why not your doting son?

ANNIE. I'm not conjuring. I'm hoping I'll remember how to fix this piece of shit.

(**ANNIE** *gestures to the GPS beacon.*)

JULIE. It isn't broken.

ANNIE. Oh really? And I suppose by some miracle you and Peter are coming to take me home right now?

JULIE. And if we were? What would you say to him?

ANNIE. I'm not having this conversation with you.

(**ANNIE** *goes to put the sunglasses and headscarf back on and discovers they're missing.*)

What – / Where are my –

(**ANNIE** *checks the water. Nothing.*)

JULIE. Would you tell him you were sorry?

ANNIE. Did you do this?

JULIE. Would you ask him to forgive you?

ANNIE. Did you distract me so you could –

(**ANNIE** *checks again. She's on the verge of tears.*)

JULIE. And if he did? Would that mean you weren't guilty?

ANNIE. Stop it! I don't want to think about Peter –

(*Behind them both,* **PETER** *turns away from the paper and maps he's pinning. He climbs one of the stepladders.*)

– when I think of Peter all I can think about is –

(**PETER** *shuffles, nervous:*)

PETER. The story of Noah and The Ark, by Peter Iversen, age ten. And a half. A long, long time ago, in a galaxy far, far away, there lived a man named Noah. He had the biggest zoo in the whole universe, with lions, and penguins, and great big elephants. Two of every kind of animal. One day, God told Noah that everyone in the land was bad, and he was going to send a flood. "That's not fair!" said Noah, "I'm not bad, and my family's not bad, and the animals haven't done anything at all!" And God saw that Noah was right, and the animals hadn't done anything at all, so God told Noah to build a really big boat for his family and all of the animals in the zoo. And then it rained for forty days and forty nights, and everybody who was bad was drowned away, and on the boat everybody was happy, until a dove came to tell them that the world was ready, and everything could begin again. The end. (**ANNIE** *claps.*) Mom? Was I good? Did I say it right?

ANNIE. You were perfect, sweetheart. Mommy is so proud of you. What do you want for a present? A new baseball glove?

(**PETER** *rushes down from the ladder but before he reaches* **ANNIE,** **JULIE** *runs to him. He lifts* **JULIE** *off the ground and spins her.*)

PETER. A kayak! You got me a kayak?

JULIE. Pete! It isn't even new. It's my old trainer.

(**ANNIE** *leans towards them, trying to capture* **PETER**'s *attention.*)

ANNIE. Lego? Ninja Turtles? A new Nintendo game?

PETER. It's perfect. When you get back this summer, we'll take the boats and just – paddle away from everything.

JULIE. I got you a GPS module, too. Maps, beacon – everything.

ANNIE. An SUV!

(**PETER** *and* **JULIE** *turn to her in astonishment.*)

PETER. Mom? You…bought me an SUV?

ANNIE. For your first year on the job. Your father and I wanted you to know just how proud of you we are.

*(**PETER** shifts uncomfortably between **JULIE** and his mother.)*

PETER. Uh – thanks, Mom.

ANNIE. You can use it to take the kayaks out to the lake.

(beat)

JULIE. No. We can't.

PETER. Jules –

ANNIE. What?

JULIE. It's an SUV, Pete.

PETER. I know. But – Jules – we shouldn't do this right now.

JULIE. Really?

ANNIE. Is there something wrong with giving my son a car for his birthday?

JULIE. Yes!

ANNIE. What is wrong with you?

PETER. Mom!

JULIE. What is wrong with you?

PETER. Jules. You aren't being fair. She means well and you're just going to upset her.

*(As the argument builds **PETER** and **JULIE** begin to circle around **ANNIE**.)*

JULIE. She means well, Pete? They blackmailed you into a life you didn't want, and now she's bought you your own private environmental disaster, and you don't want me to talk about it so she won't get her feelings hurt?

PETER. You know it isn't that simple!

JULIE. It isn't?

PETER. This is why you lost your placement with Oxfam. You have to pick your battles, Jules. Fighting all of them – all the time –

ANNIE. We researched this. We looked at safety records
  and fuel economy and emissions standards. We paid
  $45,000 for a model with very low emissions standards.
  How is a "green" vehicle some kind of crime?

JULIE. Does it use gas?

ANNIE. Oh my God!

PETER. Jules, you're being completely unreasonable. There
  are sides to this. Facets. She's doing her best with
  something very complex –

JULIE. No. It isn't complex. Complex is just what people say
  when they want to muddy up the waters.

PETER. Is that what you think I'm doing?

JULIE. Are you going to drive your shiny new SUV, Pete?

  (PETER *goes to speak but she's got him trapped.*)

  How many more years before you quit the market?

PETER. I have stopped eating meat and I bicycle to work
  and I do it for you so you don't get to judge me on this.

JULIE. You do it for me? Did you just say –

PETER. I didn't mean –

JULIE. No. You did. I have waited and waited for you to
  stand up for yourself with them. For the things you
  believe. I could never figure out why you didn't. But
  this – You don't want to.

PETER. Jules – believing in things doesn't mean making
  everybody miserable. You used to be fun. Now I can't
  even be around you without wondering what I'll do to
  set off Perfect Julie's moral compass.

JULIE. You want a moral compass, Pete? Stupid or evil, pick
  one.

PETER. What?

JULIE. That's the choice. Does she not know she's hurt-
  ing people? Or does she just not care? Because Pete
  – meaning "well" doesn't count for shit.

ANNIE. Alright. This has gotten out of control. It's just a
  car, not the end of the world – and I'm sorry if it isn't
  the best choice – but you've got to allow people the
  room to make mistakes.

JULIE. And when there's no room left for anyone? You think being kind and making allowances is going to make a difference?

PETER. Julie – you can't seriously believe what you're saying. It's crazy.

JULIE. You know what the worst part is? Her – I expected. But you – Pete – how can you know what you know and do nothing?

PETER. Because I have to live here, Julie. In the real world. Not in some dreamland where you pretend you're nineteen forever and your life isn't passing you by.

(beat)

JULIE. You know what, Mrs. Iversen? He's all yours.

(JULIE exits.)

PETER. God. Mom, I'm sorry. I can't believe she said that –

ANNIE. It's alright, Peter. Everyone gets angry. Once she's blown off some steam you'll talk –

PETER. There's nothing left to talk about. Once Julie decides she's right...

ANNIE. I'm sure she feels that way now –

PETER. No. She's already on my case about the job – about –

ANNIE. Well. Then...Maybe it's best to take a break. You can't decide to love somebody because they're right or wrong.

PETER. Yeah. No. No, of course not.

(PETER heads up right to the post-its. He slumps back against the wall.)

ANNIE. And just like that, she was gone.

(ANNIE looks around to make sure she's alone.)

How about that? Little Miss "Saves The Day"? Got anything clever to add about that?

(No sign of JULIE. ANNIE's skin and eyes are starting to hurt from the sun.)

ANNIE. *(cont.)* Not so mouthy when you aren't shoving boats and stealing sunglasses, are you?

(Still nothing. As she speaks, **ANNIE** *takes out her supplies and indulges in a celebratory treat of chocolate and graham crackers and a short sip of water.)*

He never did drive the SUV. In the end, I started using it to putter around town. And everything was lovely. For awhile. No more soy products at family dinners, and no more awkward silences when Peter and his father talked about the market. Peter even went out on a few dates with Tamara (the event planner), and Angie (the executive assistant), both of whom, I would like to add, might have made lovely fiancées, and very good mothers for my grandchildren[*].

(Upstage right, **PETER** *tidies up his tie and jacket, going through the motions.)*

But…he just didn't seem that interested. In anything. He started spending all his free time down at the marina with that blasted kayak. Still, he had a steady job that paid well, enough protein in his diet, and there was no one shooting at him in the streets of Johannesburg,[9] or deporting him from South Africa.

*(*JULIE *enters up left with a placard.* **PETER** *watches her from his side of the stage.)*

And if he was spending his nights on the Internet scanning video of protests for her face, or hopelessly re-watching that clip of her kayaking in Bolivia – well – he'd been seeing her for three years. He wasn't going to forget her overnight. He just needed to be reminded of where his life was headed before Julie – collided with it.

(Underneath **ANNIE**'s *voice the sound of a protest in a busy street has been growing.* **JULIE** *is silently yelling and waving her placard.)*

(As **ANNIE**'s *speech ends, three gunshots ring out. Silence.* **JULIE** *falls.* **PETER** *is frozen, watching her from his edge of the stage. Beat.)*

---

*See Appendix A

(JULIE pushes herself to her knees. Looks around. Checks her arms and head for blood. Slowly, deliberately, she raises her placard again, then returns to the upstage wall to continue adding post-its.)

(PETER exhales in relief. He comes downstage to lean against the kayak.)

PETER. It's okay, Mom. You don't need to take me to lunch just because I helped Dad fix the air-conditioning.

ANNIE. You had to go all the way down to the basement. And it's been so hot this summer – Thirty-eight degrees last week. *(beat)* How are you doing? You look tired.

PETER. Late nights, I guess.

ANNIE. You need to get your sleep. You're looking skinny, too. Did you eat the mashed potatoes I sent home with you last week?

PETER. Uh-huh.

ANNIE. I know you've been down, sweetie – but you'll pick up. We just need to shake you out of this – rut you're in. You should come over for Labour Day. We'll do steaks, lemonade.

PETER. Sure.

ANNIE. Sweetie.

PETER. It's fine, Mom. I guess I just thought – that after school, or after the job, that – things would be different.

ANNIE. You're in an in-between place. Once you meet someone nice, settle in – maybe some grandchildren…

PETER. I don't want to make the world any worse, Mom.

ANNIE. Grandchildren wouldn't make the world worse – you'd raise them like we raised you.

PETER. Look, Mom – some things you can't fix with barbecue and a middle-class life plan – It's fine. I'll figure something out, okay?

ANNIE. Of course, sweetie. I was just – oh dear god what's that in front of City Hall?

PETER. It's a protest, Mom.

ANNIE. Why?

PETER. They're – The government in Iran is killing protestors.[10]

ANNIE. So they're protesting for other protestors? Sometimes, Peter, this all just gets confusing.

PETER. Wait – wait – stop the car.

*(**PETER** pulls away from **ANNIE** in the kayak as though he's hopping out of a car.)*

ANNIE. Peter! What are you – ! Don't open the door – We're in traffic – ! Peter Scott Iversen!

*(**JULIE** is now standing on her stepladder, upstage left. **PETER** freezes.)*

JULIE. This is not a new story. This is the first story. They told it every year in Sunday School. There was a flood coming. Noah knew about the flood but he wasn't scared, because he was rich and could build an Ark. The world would end, but Noah would be safe. And after everyone else had been drowned the whole earth would be his, and there wouldn't even be anyone left complain about how it came to be that way. Late at night after Sunday School I would wonder about Noah's neighbours, and what they did when the rain began to fall, so fast and so thick they knew everything was ending. All those tall, dark men with their beards in wet curls and women with their sopping veils, and children with big brown eyes. Didn't anyone think of Noah? Did they come wading through the water? Calling out for help, holding their children out to be pulled into the Ark and saved? Maybe Noah believed that they were all wicked; or that if he let even one onto the boat with his family he'd have to let everyone on and there wouldn't be enough room; or that it was his boat built with his labour and his money and nobody had the right to force him to share it. But there must have been so many of them. Hoping to be saved. Clinging to the Ark as the waters rose.

Why didn't they just climb on board? I was nine or ten when I figured it out. Noah had known about the flood, so Noah had known about this, too. He had built an Ark to save himself from the flood. What had he built to save himself from them? Spears, or clubs, or arrows? Did he pour boiling oil down the sides as they tried to climb up? Or was it as simple as pushing them under the waves with his oars? What else could Noah do? There was a flood, and he had to defend his Ark. This is the lesson of Noah: The price of boarding the Ark has always been murdering the people who don't get saved, whether you do it up close and personal or from millions of miles away. Your choice is a dead body in the water or a murderer on an Ark. Unless you want to defy God. Unless you start working to stop the flood now.

PETER. Nice speech.

JULIE. Yeah. I thought it might depress the shit out of everyone in earshot. How's prosperity?

PETER. Prosperous. How's self-righteousness?

JULIE. Justified. *(beat)* Look, Pete – I've got killer jet-lag and a hard-line regime to annoy, so unless you're here to pick up a sign...

PETER. You didn't call.

JULIE. I crashed with a friend. No phone. Besides, nothing's changed.

PETER. You got deported from South Africa.

JULIE. Oh. That. People there didn't like the things I said about their mothers.

PETER. I saw the footage of the riot.

(**JULIE** *grins.*)

JULIE. Cyber-stalking? Very classy. I hear the tear gas shots were exciting.

PETER. Jesus Christ – ! They were shooting at you, Julie!

JULIE. I remember.

PETER. If they'd killed you – what would I do if they killed you? *(Beat. They don't look at each other.)* Look – After what happened, I was angry. And then for awhile I was relieved – I could get up in the morning and go to Starbucks and not worry about fair trade coffee or international graft before 9 AM –

JULIE. Sounds like that worked out then.

PETER. I was doing it just to piss you off. I'd catch myself looking for you, like you'd be across the street, or at a corner table. And I realized that what I really wanted was for you to be there, so that I could do better. So that you could be proud of me.

JULIE. You want a gold star for bicycling and recycling? It's yours, Pete. But don't pretend that it's anything but window dressing. There's a line, and we both know which side of it you're on.

PETER. Did you ever love me at all? Or was I just another pair of hands to hold a sign?

JULIE. Why are you watching footage of protests? Why do you care *so* much, whether or not I'm proud of you? Last I recall I was at a permanent disconnect from reality.

(beat)

PETER. Jules, I'm really trying here.

JULIE. *(gently)* I know you are.

(They stand, not looking at each other.)

ANNIE. *(as though she has just pulled alongside in the SUV)* Julie! How – well – I suppose *unexpected* isn't the right word for finding you at a protest –

JULIE. Mrs. Iversen. The BMW is looking flash.

ANNIE. Peter and I were picking up supplies for the barbecue. Though I suppose with what we're eating, we'll have to hope you don't picket that, too.

PETER. Stop it, Mom.

ANNIE. Oh, don't be silly. Julie knows I'm just kidding around.

JULIE. I'm sure she means well.

PETER. Jules –

JULIE. Have fun at your barbecue, Peter. Mrs. Iversen.

(*JULIE starts to leave.*)

PETER. Julie? Julie!

(*She turns.*)

Take care, Jules. Promise me.

JULIE. Sorry, Pete. If it upsets you that much I think you might have to stop cyber-stalking.

(*over her shoulder as she leaves:*)

Because if you didn't have the stomach for Johannesburg, I don't think you want to watch us in Yichang.[11]

PETER. Yichang? Jules – you aren't being serious. You can't go to the Summit. Jules! You can't go to Yichang!

(*But* **JULIE** *has returned upstage to work on the wall.* **PETER** *paces, torn between his mother and running after her.*)

ANNIE. For goodness sakes, Peter. Get in the car. You look like a crazy person.

PETER. You don't understand, Mom. Yichang –

ANNIE. Will be dangerous. Like everything she does. (*beat*) Peter. You have got to start thinking about yourself. You can't spend your life chasing after the approval of some girl who will only love you if you measure up.

PETER. I know. I know – But, Mom – you do realize that Julie – I mean – God, I know she's infuriating – but you realize she's good, right?

ANNIE. Of course she is, Peter. Everybody's good.

(**PETER** *looks at his mother for a long time. He heads upstage to keep building the wall. He stays stage right.* **JULIE** *stays stage left.*)

(*On the water, the glare is redder now.* **ANNIE** *is sunburnt, and very tired. She checks the GPS. Nothing. She forces herself to start paddling. Her movements are weary and slow.*)

(Once again, **ANNIE**'s *paddling sets* **JULIE** *and* **PETER** *in motion. They play out another series of scenes as she speaks:)*

ANNIE. *(cont.)* After that he wouldn't even come to the house for dinner. He quit the brokerage and started a job teaching kayaking down at the marina. I know, I know. I'm not a complete idiot. But your son doesn't always know what's best for him.

*(***PETER*** peels off his suit and tie, and puts on jeans and a camp t-shirt. He seems happier, but he's still looking over at* **JULIE** *working on the wall.)*

He didn't want to eat his vegetables, and he didn't want to spend his Thursday nights at a math tutor's, but he grew up big and strong and with a math average that got him into a good university. And maybe he wanted to be a inventor, or an army medic, or Han Solo when he was ten –

*(***ANNIE*** slumps, then forces herself to keep paddling. ***JULIE*** goes over charts and makes notes, chatting on a cell with other activists. When she folds up her phone, she looks over at* **PETER** *working on the wall.)*

– but a business degree will get you a stable job with a good dental plan and a solid retirement package, which will allow you to buy a house, which will give you a place to keep your wife and children while you force them to eat their vegetables and go to math tutors and that is a solid foundation for future happiness.

*(***ANNIE***'s movements are irregular, feeble, but she forces herself to keep going. ***PETER*** watches ***JULIE*** work. He writes a letter and seals it.)*

You want that for your children. Everything you can give them. Noah wouldn't have let his children say: "Hey Dad, we're not getting on your crazy boat –

JULIE. Noah again?

(The paddle slips from **ANNIE**'s *grasp. She scrambles to catch it before it slips into the water.)*

ANNIE. "Because you're mistreating these animals and you choosing us for salvation is nepotism!"

(*JULIE drifts down to the kayak. On the water, the sun is setting.* **ANNIE** *shivers.*)

JULIE. I get the fascination. The great boat that carries us safely to our new beginning. All our sins washed away. But it's a child's story. And it isn't yours. *(beat)* You know, people dying of exposure? Near the end they crawl under leaves or into holes to hide, even from the people trying to save them. Sometimes they're found, curled up and cold, a few feet from where someone passed by, calling their name. And that's you, Mrs. Iversen. Crawling into someone else's story. Hoping you'll die before you have to tell your own.

ANNIE. Really? Because I don't think you'd like my story. In my story, a little girl who thinks she's better than everyone else wants my son to go to dangerous places with dirty water and corrupt governments to help people too weak to help themselves. She's a naïve, stupid little girl who thinks the world is a fairytale with good people and bad people and nobody in between, and she gets in over her head and leaves nothing behind but the wreckage of my family!*

JULIE. Oh, so this is my fault now?

(*JULIE shoves the kayak.* **ANNIE** *wobbles.*)

ANNIE. You put those ideas in his head. Made him feel responsible for things that had nothing to do with him. Had him looking at every goddamn thing in terms of right and wrong.

JULIE. Told him he had to choose.

ANNIE. Yes!

JULIE. I never lied to him, though, did I?

(*JULIE heads downstage left and begins to pack up a backpack. Upstage right,* **PETER** *does too.*)

ANNIE. Hello, Julie.

---

* See Appendix B

JULIE. Mrs. Iversen? What are you doing here?

ANNIE. This is a very interesting – house?

JULIE. Commune.

ANNIE. Ah.

JULIE. Look, Mrs. Iversen. I'm sure you've got some reason you think is a good one for being here, but I'm shipping out in about eight hours –

ANNIE. Peter's worried about you –

JULIE. Well, that's Pete for you. I'm still going.

ANNIE. I went to see him for breakfast yesterday. There was a visitor's VISA from the Chinese consulate in his mail.

(beat)

JULIE. You know that opening your adult son's mail is illegal, right? Also, creepy.

ANNIE. Do you love my son?

JULIE. Oh god.

ANNIE. If you love my son, how can you drag him into something that might get him killed?

JULIE. Is there anything I can say that might get you to leave?

ANNIE. No! I've seen that footage from Johannesburg. With gas, and billy clubs, and rubber bullets. And China will be worse – they're talking about imprisoning protestors as environmental terrorists. Do you understand that, you idiot girl?

JULIE. Do you understand it, Mrs. Iversen? The Chinese government is pumping more greenhouse gases and carcinogens into the air than anyone, even America: The effects are already disastrous. And if you say what they're doing is wrong, they threaten to imprison you.

ANNIE. They *can* imprison you. They could kill you. They could kill Peter.

JULIE. And you think I'm not terrified? I don't have some martyr complex. I don't want to die. Mostly, Mrs. Iversen, I want to finish my English degree, and maybe take my playboat down some good rides in the summer. But if they can say right is wrong and kill anyone who disagrees, then how am I supposed to be safe? In my classes? In my boat? So no. This first. This has to come first.

ANNIE. Please.

JULIE. Mrs. Iversen?

ANNIE. I know I can't convince you. I don't have studies and facts and eyewitnesses and videos. But I love my son. More than right or wrong. I can't just let you take him. I want to stage a protest. Right here. This is my protest. I'll make banners, and hold signs. If you ask him, he'll go. Of course he'll go, he's a twenty-four year-old boy and you're a pretty girl who acts like she's here to save the world. But you don't love him –

(**JULIE** *bristles, but* **ANNIE** *keeps going.*)

– and I do. You have the whole world to save. Peter is my whole world. Please don't take my son away from me.

(*beat*)

JULIE. I haven't asked him to come with me, and I won't.

ANNIE. Thank you.

JULIE. He wasn't going to choose me, you know. I thought he might, when we started. When I thought it would take six months to change the world and then I'd just – come home. Peter was my way home. He would write or call or smile – and even when I was so scared and angry that it hurt to breathe – I'd remember that there was still a world with iced-coffee and kisses and sunshine in the kitchen window because it was waiting there, in Peter's voice. In Peter's face. But then six months became a year, and then two, and three. And I started to see it: that I couldn't change anything. I would wake up beside Peter at 4:00 AM and everything would be unrecognizable: My life, my plans. It was like someone had filled the room with water. Filled the world with water. It wasn't my world. It was theirs. It was yours. And there was no room for me to even breathe in it. It would never change, and I'd never be able to stop. Never come home. Not even to Peter. I'd lost him before we even met. *(beat)* I think you should go now, Mrs. Iversen.

ANNIE. Yes. Yes, of course.

(JULIE *finishes packing and returns to the upstage wall. She goes back to pinning up papers and plans.)*

(Out on the water, the wind is picking up. ANNIE *shivers and rubs her arms, trying to keep warm.)*

(PETER *finishes packing and heads downstage.)*

PETER. Camping? You want to go camping?

ANNIE. I thought we could spend some time together. I barely see you these days.

PETER. You hate camping.

ANNIE. I don't hate it. I like lots of things about – I like S'mores. And – I've already got your kayak strapped to the top of the BMW, you can splash around along the Credit –

PETER. I can't.

ANNIE. Of course you can. Your classes finish up tomorrow. We'll have plenty of time.

PETER. No, Mom. I can't. I'm – uh – going on a trip.

ANNIE. A trip? You didn't say anything about a vacation. Where are you going?

PETER. Okay. Don't overreact. But I'm going to Yichang. I'm going to Summit.

ANNIE. Well, you'll just have to cancel.

PETER. What?

ANNIE. We can't change the dates – I've got your old kayak all ready to go, and a deposit on the campsite, and – and – supplies packed. The marshmallows will get stale.

PETER. Mom, I appreciate that you've gone to the trouble, but –

ANNIE. Your father will be so disappointed if you don't come along. He'll be stuck out there with me –

PETER. Mom.

ANNIE. It's so dangerous there.

PETER. I'll be fine.

ANNIE. This is not fine, Peter. *(beat)* You're risking your safety to go chasing after a girl who – who doesn't care about you.

PETER. This isn't about –

ANNIE. Who doesn't call you.

PETER. She –

ANNIE. Who hasn't asked you to come with her, has she?

PETER. No. She hasn't. I'm not doing this because of Julie.

ANNIE. Of course you are. *(beat)* I didn't want to tell you. I went to see her.

PETER. You what?

ANNIE. I was afraid she'd push you into doing something dangerous. When I got there she was packing up – getting ready to leave – with another young man.

PETER. Oh.

ANNIE. I know that must be hard for you to hear. But I thought it would be better than following her all the way to China just to find out. *(beat)* Peter, are you alright?

PETER. I – uh – I think maybe I need to sit down. *(He sits down, then stands up again immediately.)* I'm sorry.

ANNIE. Peter. There's no need for that. Some things just happen.

PETER. Some things happen because you let them.

ANNIE. What are you – ?

PETER. I'm sorry. I have to go. Now.

ANNIE. Peter Scott Iversen –

PETER. You're not talking me out of this, Mom.

ANNIE. Peter, even if you love her –

PETER. Of course I love her. I think I've been in love with her from that first stupid YouTube video in Bolivia. I just didn't know why. She missed three term papers to be a part of that protest and didn't sleep for a week to catch up. And when they diverted the river anyway she wrote appeals and editorials – she kept trying even when it was hopeless. Why wouldn't you love someone for that? Why wouldn't that be the best reason to love someone? I need her to know I understand that. And I need to stand up too. I'm sorry, I have to go.

ANNIE. Peter, if you leave – if you put me through this – I swear – I – I will never even speak to you again.

PETER. Mom –

ANNIE. Don't bother coming home.

(beat)

PETER. Alright then.

*(**PETER** returns to the upstage wall.)*

*(On the water, the wind is getting worse and so is **ANNIE**'s shivering.)*

ANNIE. Don't bother coming home. Stupid thing to say. The soap opera cliché version of the last thing you say to your son before he runs off to China after his ex-girlfriend and both of them die.

(She checks the GPS beacon again. Nothing. She shakes it. Still nothing.)

Goddamn this piece of shit!

*(**ANNIE** flings the GPS beacon away.)*

JULIE. That was productive.

ANNIE. Oh, go rescue a puppy.

*(**ANNIE** takes out the cracker sleeve and the water bottle, and starts gnawing on a cracker.)*

I bet you just love this. Don't you?

*(**JULIE**, and then **PETER**, begin to circle in on the kayak.)*

JULIE. The camping trip was your idea.

ANNIE. I was supposed to be on it with my son.

JULIE. You think Peter would be better off here? With you?

ANNIE. He wouldn't be dead.

JULIE. What are you planning to do when the graham crackers run out?

(The wind is still rising. In the distance there's a crack of thunder. JULIE looks over her shoulder.)

Looks like we're about to find out.

(She shoves the kayak. ANNIE wobbles.)

ANNIE. Stop that. You'll make me –

(ANNIE struggles to stow the water and crackers to get ready for the storm. From the opposite side, PETER shoves the kayak.)

Please, please don't!

JULIE. C'mon, Mrs. Iversen! You were just gonna keep making excuses. Telling stories. Let's skip straight to that Eskimo roll.

(JULIE shoves again. Harder. The crackers and the water bottle go flying.)

ANNIE. No!

(PETER shoves. JULIE shoves. ANNIE tries to fend them off with her paddle. The wind is howling and now there are ominous flickers and rumbles on the horizon.)

JULIE. You never cared before! You just let it happen! Let everything tip. Right. Over.

ANNIE. I said leave me alone!

(ANNIE paddles away. JULIE calls after her:)

JULIE. You are alone, Mrs. Iversen. Doesn't matter how far you paddle, you're still in the same boat! *(JULIE laughs, maniacally, painfully.)* We're all in the same boat!

(The storm. The thunder and lightning grow worse. ANNIE paddles desperately. A dark moment, when the kayak is visible again, PETER is in it instead of ANNIE. ANNIE watches from the side as he struggles with the waves and the water. Another dark moment, and JULIE is in the kayak. ANNIE watches from the opposite side as JULIE paddles for all she's worth, amazed by the storm. Flash. Darkness. ANNIE is in the kayak again. PETER and JULIE are gone.)

*(The storm becomes heavy, relentless rain. ANNIE hud-
dles in the kayak. Miserable.)*

*(Upstage, where JULIE and PETER have been pinning
papers and post-its, the collage has become a shape on the
back wall. What was simply a scattering of papers has
developed into the forms of continents: North America,
South America, Europe, Asia, Africa.)**

MALE NEWSCASTER. *(recorded voice)* The G8 Environmental
Summit continues today in Yichang, China, where protests persist despite government restrictions and the
unprecedented series of storms which has kicked off
south-east China's rainy season.

ANNIE. There was a dam. That's the part of Noah's story
that isn't in the bible. There was a dam. Miles high,
miles thick. And behind it was all the water in the
world. It was made of the best brick for hundreds of
miles around, and because it was easy, all the people
in the valley took their bricks from its sides. They did
it for centuries. The walls were miles high, and miles
thick, and they would never run out.

*(From their opposite sides of the stage, PETER and JULIE
enter behind ANNIE. They wear rain slickers and carry
placards.)*

FEMALE NEWSCASTER. *(recorded voice)* Three protestors have
been hospitalized in skirmishes with private security
forces here in Yichang, and tensions are rising, as the
Chinese government insists protestors disperse immediately, or face imprisonment and/or deportation.

ANNIE. Noah took the bricks, just like everyone else, but
one day, farther than he had ever gone before, he
noticed a trickle of water, thin as the pulse in a little
girl's wrist, running down from somewhere above.
Noah ran home crying that the dam was about to
burst. But the dam was miles high, and miles thick,
and no one believed him.

---

* See Appendix A

(PETER and JULIE step towards each other. He pushes back his hood. She pushes back hers. JULIE holds her face up to feel the rain.)

MALE NEWSCASTER. *(recorded voice)* The landmark summit is taking place in the shadow of China's Three Gorges Dam. Several protestors have already been arrested while vandalizing the dam itself.

ANNIE. And when Noah tried to stop people from taking the bricks, they laughed at him. They said if the brick was really so important, he should take the bricks from his own home, and use them to save the dam.

(PETER waves. JULIE waves back. They start moving slowly towards each other.)

FEMALE NEWSCASTER. *(recorded voice)* A controversy now in Yichang, where Environmental talks have been suspended, while accusations fly that Chinese and American delegates are sabotaging negotiations. Protestors are gathered here in front of the Yichang Hotel, where the American delegation is staying, and we're just now getting word of an incident –

ANNIE. So Noah took down his home, brick by brick, and his wife and sons cried. But even after Noah had put all the bricks back the little pulse of water didn't stop because the dam had been built long ago and Noah didn't really know how it worked but he knew that the water was still coming so he – he built a boat and he – uh – filled it with two – of every kind of animal and he prepared places in it for his – sons – and – and – their wives and – then – and then –

(PETER and JULIE are face-to-face in front of the upstage wall. The rain is coming harder now.)

MALE NEWSCASTER. *(recorded voice)*: A massive flood has breached the Three Gorges Dam in China, putting the Yangtze Valley under at least five meters of water. Early reports suggest that the dam was weakened by a small earthquake in the early hours of the morning, and subsequently burst. Hardest hit, of course, is the small city of Yichang, where negotiations for the G8 Environmental Summit were taking place. Unconfirmed reports seem to indicate that most of the city was destroyed in the dam's initial collapse, and current projections place the death toll for Yichang alone at 4.1 million.

*(Behind **ANNIE**, **PETER** and **JULIE** take each other's hands. Over them, the post-it map of the world tumbles down in a cascade of paper.[12] Once the cascade finishes, they are gone.)*

ANNIE. And then the world ended.

*(After a moment she looks around for **JULIE** and **PETER**. Nothing.)*

It was supposed to be me. Isn't that how it happens? The flood comes and it washes away the people who are guilty. I never did anything but what everyone else did. I drove the cars they drove, I ate the things they ate, if all those people were going to die why wasn't I the one who went with them? If the flood was going to come it was supposed to take me. Not my son.

(Beat. She's alone in the dark.)

Not my son.

(beat)

It wasn't long before they figured it out. That it wasn't just Yichang. Or the Yangtze Valley. Or South-East China.

FEMALE NEWSCASTER. *(recorded voice)* With heavy monsoon rains continuing, India and Pakistan are threatened with yet another series of devastating flash floods[13] –

ANNIE. That something, somewhere had reached a tipping point.

MALE NEWSCASTER. *(recorded voice)* The death toll in southern Brazil has risen to over 1000 now, with mudslides[14] burying homes, roads and powerlines, leaving rescue workers helpless –

ANNIE. That the rain would just keep coming. That the water was rising. Everywhere.

FEMALE NEWSCASTER. *(recorded voice)* A coalition of African nations including Uganda, Ethiopia and Sudan are establishing an international task force[15] to oversee immediate relief and assess the damage to food and water reserves in the wake of what some are now calling "The Great Flood" –

(Underneath ANNIE's speeches, the news reports have grown faint, becoming little more than a buzz of static.)

ANNIE. I'd driven out to Peter's apartment – I couldn't sit there with Herb listening to the news reports –

MALE NEWSCASTER. *(recorded voice)* …more than a fifth of the area underwater…

ANNIE. When I got on the 401 to drive back home, the traffic was stopped. For miles.

FEMALE NEWSCASTER. …widespread reports of looting…no signs of the water receding…

ANNIE. The rain was still coming. You could see the roadside ditches filling. What do you do when you're stopped on the 401 and the water is slowly rising? On the radio you could hear them talking about getting to higher ground – but after Yichang I think we all knew that higher ground wasn't going to help anyone.

(The static of the news reports fades away.)

When the water got past the wheels, I remembered Peter's kayak. It was still in the back with the camping supplies. So I took my graham crackers and chocolate and marshmallows, and I started paddling home. A few people chased me, I'd never really paddled before – but after awhile I looked back and I couldn't see them. No men. No cars. Nothing but water.

(Just faintly, a beeping begins.)

ANNIE. *(cont.)* I thought I could just paddle until I found
– someone. That sooner or later a motorboat, or a
yacht, or an ocean liner, or something would appear
on the horizon. Or I'd hear someone calling and I'd
call back. Or – I don't know – I'd be struck with some
great light from a rescue boat. But after a few days that
stopped seeming likely. I thought, maybe if I could get
the GPS to work –

*(**ANNIE** looks around but the GPS module is nowhere to
be seen.)*

– that I could go home. I thought that I'd like to get
home before I – to see if Herb was – to the house I
raised my son in, and the backyard I – I wanted to see
what was left of the life I killed them for. But I guess
this is it. One stretch of water is as good as any, and I'm
goddamn sick of S'mores.

*(**ANNIE** empties out the kayak. Littering her effects all
over the water.)*

It just seems abrupt, you know. After all this. One
minute you're sitting there. The next you're upside
down and underwater.

*(Faintly, the beeping continues, the beeps growing closer
and closer together.)*

That video of Julie in Bolivia, following the river down –
She's so small – and there's so much water. It wrenches
that little kayak around, throws her over waterfalls.

*(A sound like rushing water joins the beeping. Both grow
gradually louder as **ANNIE** continues to speak.)*

She's falling and all around her tonnes of water are
falling too. There's this one awful drop – she falls for
so long, and the kayak disappears into the white and
the water, and then it floats out beneath the water-
fall upside down. And the camera shakes, and along
the river you can hear her friends screaming for her:
"Julie-Julie-Julie" and you're terrified too, even though
you don't really like her. You knew she was tiny, but

you never thought of how she was barely a hundred pounds of little bones and pigtails against all the water and rock in the world, and suddenly you're crying too: "Julie-Julie-Julie" at that stupid square of video on your computer screen because looking at an overturned kayak drifting away you suddenly knew that there was no hope for anyone at all in the world if it's the kind of world that would drown Julie dead.

(beat)

ANNIE. *(cont.)* And that's the moment she rolls the kayak back over, pops up laughing and waving and you hate her as much as you've ever hated anyone but she is a miracle, that tiny little girl laughing and waving and breathing and happy and *good.* And you're laughing and crying and waving back at your computer screen because she did it. She saved herself.

(The sound of crashing water and the beeping, having reached a fever pitch, suddenly stop.)

I wonder if that's how it was for them at the end. Just a crashing of white and water. No time even to be afraid. To realize the miracle would never happen.

*(**ANNIE** takes a deep breath, and prepares to roll the kayak over.)*

VOICE. *(from a great distance.)* Mrs. Iversen?

*(**ANNIE** looks around, startled. Nothing.)*

*(**ANNIE** takes another breath, readies herself again.)*

(louder) Mrs. Iversen?

*(**ANNIE** looks around again.)*

(She takes a final breath, but stops for a moment, listening.)

*(Unmistakable. **JULIE** on a loud speaker.)* Mrs. Iversen?

(There is a long, terrible pause.)

ANNIE. *(whispered)* Julie? *(Beat. Louder.)* Julie? *(Beat. Screaming.)* JULIE!

(An enormous light strikes **ANNIE** *from on high, as from the deck of an ocean freighter.* **JULIE**'s *voice comes down with the light.)*

JULIE. It's okay Mrs. Iversen. We're coming down to get you. Pete! Get the ropes, your mom saved your goddamn kayak!

*(***ANNIE*** *doesn't hear* **PETER**'s *reply, but at his name her face twists into an expression of terrible joy, and she folds her head into her hands, sobbing in the great beam of light.)*

End

NOTES

1. Many versions of this African-American Spiritual are available in the public domain. For the version I listened to as a child, please see: Cavoukian, Raffi. "Who Built The Ark?" *The Singable Song Collection.*

2. As a staging recommendation, both Peter and Julie should appear faded, perhaps even a little watery, to keep the focus of staging on Annie.

3. The Tuichi river is located in the Madidi National Park in the north of Bolivia, and is a favorite for white-water rafting and kayaking expeditions. The conflict between IWL and Greenpeace over the Tuichi River is fictional, but was modeled in part on the "Cocambamba Water Wars" that took place in Bolivia between January and April 2000.

4. *An Inconvenient Truth.* Dir. Davis Guggenheim. Perf. Al Gore. 2006.

5. Referring to the Free Tibet Protests leading up to the Beijing Olympics in 2008.

6. Referring to Greenpeace's ongoing campaign against deforestation caused by the Palm Kernel Oil industry in South East Asia.

7. Referring to Greenpeace's ongoing campaign against the farming of GMO rice in the Philippines.

8. Referring to Greenpeace's ongoing campaign to save the endangered Japanese dugong, by opposing the relocation of a U.S. military air base into the creatures' only remaining habitat.

9. Referring to the Anti-Xenopobia Protests and violent riots that occurred in Johannesburg in 2008-2009.

10. Referring to the protests that followed the controversial election of Mahmoud Ahmadinejad in Iran, where at least 36 protestors were killed.

11. The fictional Environmental Summit that takes place in Yichang is modeled in part on the Environmental Summit that took place in Copenhagen in 2010, and in part on the WTO Protests that took place in Seattle in 1999.

12. The tumbling paper map of the world is most simply achieved with two flats of identical size. A series of blunt nails in the desired shape should protrude from the surface of the rear flat, and should correspond to a series of holes in the front flat. As Peter and Julie build the map of post-its, they simply place the post-its' adhesive strips across the holes in the front flat. To cause the map to tumble, two stagehands simply push the front flat flush against the rear flat, pushing the blunt nails through the holes and dislodging the post-its. This effect can be enhanced by varying the length of the blunt nails in the rear flat, and/or by adding a drop of additional post-its from the grid.

13. This series of fictional floods is based in part on the devastating floods that struck Pakistan in late July of 2010.

14. These fictional mudslides are based in part on the floods that struck Brazil in January of 2011.
15. This series of fictional floods is based in part on the series of floods that struck seventeen African nations (including those mentioned) in late September of 2007.

APPENDIX A: VIDEO PROJECTIONS

Earlier drafts of *Kayak* contained a series of video projections intended to help contextualize Annie and Julie's struggles in the scope of a larger world. Included here is a complete list of the projections and the stage directions that accompanied them:

Preset Video:
A series of shots of small children playing in a wading pool.

Video Section #1:
(Continued from page 14)

ANNIE. I definitely couldn't stand her. Four years and she never stopped calling me *Mrs.* Iversen.

> *(Upstage, **PETER** and **JULIE** stretch out a white, rectangular banner that becomes a projection surface.)*

> *(During **ANNIE**'s speech, video of **JULIE** in her kayak at the protest plays. **JULIE** waves happily at the camera. Little kayaks shoot down the rapids. **JULIE** and other kayakers hold up banners and throw peace signs. **JULIE** does Eskimo roll after Eskimo roll.)*

The next time I saw Julie, she was on Peter's laptop. He was home for Christmas and he had video of the little nitwit kayaking down that river as part of her protest. She'd actually gone…Herb and I ate turkey sandwiches for two weeks to finish the leftovers.

> *(The video ends. **PETER** and **JULIE** take down the banner, and return upstage to build their wall of social issues with posters and post-its.)*

Now I recognize that what Julie was doing was – good…

Video Section #2:
(Continued from page 26)

ANNIE. …both of whom, I would like to add, might have made lovely fiancées, and very good mothers for my grandchildren.

> *(By himself, **PETER** tacks up the banner that served as the video screen.)*

But…he just didn't seem that interested…and there was no one shooting at him in the streets of Johannesburg,[9] or deporting him from South Africa.

(JULIE *enters up left with a placard.* PETER *watches her from his side of the stage.*)

(*On the makeshift screen, video footage of protests is playing. People yelling. Barricades. Riot cops.*)

ANNIE. (*cont.*) And if he was spending his nights on the Internet scanning video of protests for her face... He just needed to be reminded of where his life was headed before Julie – collided with it.

(*Underneath* ANNIE*'s voice the sound of a protest in a busy street has been growing.*)

(JULIE *is silently yelling and waving her placard. The protest footage grows more and more violent. Tear gas. Arrests.*)

(*As* ANNIE*'s speech ends, three gunshots ring out. The video snaps off. Silence.* JULIE *falls.* PETER *is frozen, watching her from his edge of the stage. Beat.*)

(JULIE *pushes herself to her knees. Looks around. Checks her arms and head for blood. Slowly, deliberately, she raises her placard again, returning upstage to take down the makeshift screen and continue work on the wall.*)

(PETER *exhales in relief. He comes downstage to lean against the kayak.*)

Video Section #3:
(*Continued from page 40*)

(*...What was simply a scattering of papers has developed into the forms of continents: North America, South America, Europe, Asia, Africa. To each side of the map of the world,* JULIE *and* PETER*, wearing rain slickers, are pinning up white banners to serve as makeshift screens on their opposite sides of the stage. As each newscaster speaks, protest footage, and footage from past environmental summits plays on the screens.*)

MALE NEWSCASTER. (*recorded voice*) The G8 Environmental Summit continues today in Yichang...

ANNIE. …The walls were miles high, and miles thick, and they would never run out.

(PETER and JULIE finish tacking up the screens, pick up placards, and turn to face each other.)

FEMALE NEWSCASTER. *(recorded voice)* Three protestors have been hospitalized in skirmishes…

ANNIE. …but he knew that the water was still coming so he – he built a boat and he – uh – filled it with two – of every kind of animal and he prepared places in it for his – sons – and – and – their wives and – then – and then –

(As ANNIE begins to falter, the images on the screens begin to blip and fail.)

(PETER and JULIE are face-to-face in front of the upstage wall. The rain is coming harder now.)

MALE NEWSCASTER. *(recorded voice)* A massive flood has breached the Three Gorges Dam in China…place the death toll for Yichang alone at 4.1 million.

(During the preceding speech, the blipping video has shifted to news reports of floods. The screens flash with rising water, houses being carried away.)

(Behind ANNIE, PETER and JULIE take each other's hands. Over them, the post-it map of the world tumbles down in a cascade of paper.[12] Once the cascade finishes, they are gone.)

(The video screens have gone dark.)

ANNIE. And then the world ended…It wasn't long before they figured it out. That it wasn't just Yichang. Or the Yangtze Valley. Or South-East China.

(The images of floods return to the screens.)

FEMALE NEWSCASTER. *(recorded voice)* With heavy monsoon rains continuing, India and Pakistan are threatened with yet another…and assess the damage to food and water reserves in the wake of what some are now calling "The Great Flood" –

*(Underneath **ANNIE**'s speeches, the news reports have gorwn faint, becoming little more than a buzz of static.)*

(The continuing images of devastation fade out gradually, with the buzz of the new reports.)

ANNIE. I'd driven out to Peter's apartment – I couldn't sit there with Herb...I think we all knew that higher ground wasn't going to help anyone.

(The screens have gone dark. The static of the news reports fades away.)

Post-set Video:

The series of shots from Julie's protest at the Tuichi river.

APPENDIX B: WE'RE ALL IN THE SAME BOAT

For *Kayak's* Winnipeg production in Femfest 2010, the director, Hope MacIntyre requested that a joke told by Julie in an earlier draft be preserved in order to add a little levity to the later sections of the play. I have included the alternate text here:

(Continued from page 33)

ANNIE. …gets in over her head and leaves nothing behind but the wreckage of my family!

(beat)

JULIE. Want to hear a joke?

ANNIE. Of course. That makes perfect sense.

JULIE. On the first day of the voyage, the lions came to Noah and said: "We're hungry. We demand to be allowed to eat the cows." Noah refused, and the lions went away growling and rumbling. On the second day of the voyage, the cows came to Noah and said: "The lions are planning on eating us! We demand they be made to walk the plank!" Noah refused, and the cows went away huffing and puffing. By the third day of the voyage, everything was in uproar: the rabbits needed more space because they were breeding, the horses had a vendetta against the zebras, and the entire water supply tasted like hippo. Every single animal had come to Noah to complain. And so Noah pulled on his long white beard and thought and thought – and do you know what he told them?

ANNIE. I give up.

JULIE. He said: There's just no help for it, *we're all in the same boat.*

(JULIE begins to drift downstage.)

ANNIE. We're all in the same boat. That's funny. (*She starts to laugh. But her laughter has a sad, almost hysterical tinge to it.*) We're all in the same boat. We're all in the same boat.

(JULIE begins to pack up a backpack. Upstage right, PETER does too.)

Hello, Julie…

ABOUT THE AUTHOR

Jordan Hall is an emerging artist whose work has been dubbed "stellar, insightful" by *Plank Magazine*, "thoughtful" by CBC Radio, and "vivid, memorable" by NOW. Her writing for the stage includes her short works *Red, The Second Last Man on Earth, Annie & Izzy*, and *Asleep at the Wheel*, as well as her full-length play, *Kayak*.

Jordan's plays have been produced across Canada, most recently at the 2010 Femfest and Summerworks Festivals. She is developing her newest work, *Travelling Light*, as an Associate with the Playwrights Theatre Centre.

As a dramaturg, Jordan recently worked on the Dora Award-winning *Belle of Winnipeg* with Keystone Theatre, and works as a mentor for UBC's Booming Ground program. Find her at www.jordanhall.ca.

OTHER TITLES AVAILABLE FROM SAMUEL FRENCH

CLOSURE

Ron Blicq

Drama / 4m, 3f / Unit Set

Donald Barlow, who lives in Nottingham, England, decides to search for his father who, he has discovered, was a visiting Canadian serviceman during World War II. Following his mother's death, Donald engages a search agency to find his father (Gordon Devereaux) and establish contact. But when the agency does find Devereaux, the elderly man vehemently denies his involvement with Donald's mother and categorically refuses to meet the man who claims to be his son.

Donald's journalist daughter Claire refuses to give up and, using her married name, flies to Canada to meet and interview Devereaux. She takes her nine-year-old son with her (who actually is Devereaux's great-grandson) and a unique and unexpected friendship develops between the crusty old man and the boy. Although Claire had not intended to reveal the connection between them, she now privately telephones her father and suggests he fly to Canada. Yet her secret plan is shattered when the boy tells Devereaux things about his family, from which the old man deduces the connection and recognizes he has been duped. This sets in motion a vicious and seemingly irreversible conflict between Claire and Devereaux.

The two men do eventually face each other, but both are angry and unforgiving.

Winner of the 2008 Samuel French Canadian Playwrights Competition

"How closure is finally achieved makes this a gripping drama of four generations – and how the youngest can bring out the best in the oldest."
- The Visitor, Guernsey, UK

OTHER TITLES AVAILABLE FROM SAMUEL FRENCH

MAPLE LODGE

Colleen Curran

Comedy / 2m, 3f

Heather, Dennis and Tara are opening their cottage, Maple Lodge, for the summer and are expecting their formidable mother. The three, a college administrator, a pharmacist and a twice divorced TV anchorwoman have been coming to Maple Lodge all of their lives and Tara assures everyone that this summer will be the same as always once this weekend is over. She is wrong. Everything changes with the arrival an exotic stranger. In the meantime, Mother has won a Suitcase Dance to Mexico and will miss the big event Tara is hosting: the raising of a covered bridge to replace the beloved one burned to the ground by the Kingman brothers twenty five years ago. Her cochairman on the bridge committee, a local lumberman, just happens to be in love with Heather. Maple Lodge has kept many secrets, but they all come out this weekend.

Winner of the 1999 Samuel French Canadian Playwrights Contest

OTHER TITLES AVAILABLE FROM SAMUEL FRENCH

THAT DARN PLOT

David Belke

Comedy / 4m, 2f / Int.

Mark W. Transom, one of Canada's greatest playwrights, is at the end of his rope. In order to fulfill his contract to artistic director and old friend Jo Harber, he has to create a play in one night or lose everything. Half asleep and half drunk, Transom starts putting theatrical personalities he knows into a simple comedy about putting on a play. As the characters come to life before his eyes, the play seems to be progressing well until, unbidden and without warning, Transom's son Lloyd appears as a character and the play takes on a life of its own. As the playwright struggles to maintain the upper hand, the out of control writing process brings him closer and closer to the heart of his estrangement with his son. Hilarious and heartfelt, *That Darn Plot* is a comedy about playwriting, rehearsals, rewriting and rehabilitating reality as well as a sympathetic look at a creative writer who is unable to connect with the people around him, including his only child.

Winner of the 2000 Samuel French Canadian Playwriting Contest.

OTHER TITLES AVAILABLE FROM SAMUEL FRENCH

$38,000 FOR A FRIENDLY FACE

Kristin Shepherd

Comedy / 1m, 6f, plus extras / Interior

$38,000 For A Friendly Face takes place in our time, in a small town where Bronwyn Bain lived out the last years of her life. Her two daughters, Jane and Annie, arrive less than enthusiastically for their mother's Celebration of Life, not having seen their mother in years. The town's funeral home is run by Matt, who struggles to create a decent ending for Bronwyn and her daughters, and by The Last Supper Committee, a number of women responsible for the meals for funeral events. Preparations for the Celebration of Life deteriorate on every front. It becomes apparent that Bronwyn Bain was not well loved, and that there may be no guests. In the kitchen, The Last Supper Committee members, along with Alison, a young woman who does not leave after delivering flowers, hurl toward their own meal-destroying confrontations around the subject of death. The Celebration is saved, initially, by the storytelling of Alison and The Last Supper Committee. In the end, however, the day is saved by the understanding that none of us gets it right—in life or death.

Winner of the 2007 Samuel French Canadian Playwrights Contest.

OTHER TITLES AVAILABLE FROM SAMUEL FRENCH

A YEAR IN THE DEATH OF EDDIE JESTER

T. Gregory Argall

Comedy / 4m, 3f / Unit Set

Stand up comic Eddie Jester has been mugged and is comatose. His disembodied spirit offers up jokes and commentary on the events transpiring in his hospital room, including the simultaneous visit to his bedside of his wife and his girlfriend and some nonmedical doctor/nurse activities. Eddie's semi posthumous examination of life, love and human relationships provides funny and poignant insights while the duplicity of his agent, revelations about his father and the births of two children demonstrate to Eddie that sometimes even your own life carries on without you.

Winner of the 2002 Samuel French Canadian Playwrights Contest.